HOGG, HOGG, & HOG

margie palatini

Simon & Schuster Books for Young Readers
New York   London   Toronto   Sydney

SIMON & SCHUSTER BOOKS FOR YOUNG READERS
An imprint of Simon & Schuster Children's Publishing Division
1230 Avenue of the Americas, New York, New York 10020
Copyright © 2011 by Margie Palatini

SIMON & SCHUSTER BOOKS FOR YOUNG READERS
is a trademark of Simon & Schuster, Inc.
For information about special discounts for bulk
purchases, please contact Simon & Schuster Special
Sales at 1-866-506-1949 or
business@simonandschuster.com.
The Simon & Schuster Speakers Bureau can
bring authors to your live event. For more
information or to book an event, contact
the Simon & Schuster Speakers Bureau
at 1-866-248-3049 or visit our website
at www.simonspeakers.com.
Book design by Lucy Ruth Cummins
The text for this book is set in
Excelsior.
The illustrations for this book are
rendered digitally.
Manufactured in China • 0810 SCP
2 4 6 8 10 9 7 5 3 1
CIP data for this book is available from
the Library of Congress.
ISBN 978-1-4424-0322-2

Acknowledgments
To David, with
thanks and
appreciation.

IN THE MIDDLE OF
THE BIG CITY,
ON THE TOP FLOOR OF
THE BIGGEST BUILDING,
IT'S BIG BUSINESS AT . . .

"Hogg, Hogg, and Hog . . .
please hold.
"Hogg, Hogg, and Hog . . .
please hold.
"Sorry, Hogg, Hogg, *or*
Hog *cannot* be disturbed."

They are *very* **BIG PIGS.**

Hogg,
Hogg,
and
Hog
have
everyone
in
the
BIG CITY
OINKING!

"**OINK!** What an *idea!*"

"Amazing! Genius! *Brilliant!*"

"Hogg, Hogg, *or* Hog . . . *how* did you think of **OINK?**"

"*When* did you think of **OINK?**"

"*Where* did you think of **OINK?**"

"*Why* **OINK?**"

"*Who* **OINKED** first?"

"*What's* the next **BIG OINK?**"

". . . Is it *true* you have a movie deal?"

ING NEWS . . . HOGG NEWS CONFERENCE ... BREAKING NEWS

OINK OINK OINK. OINK. OINK. OINK OINK OI

Yes, Hogg, Hogg, *and* Hog were the most *famous*, fabulous, successful Big Pigs to ever leave the farm and make it in the **BIG CITY.**

And then, one day . . .
people just got plain old tired of oinking.

On the top floor of the **BIGGEST BUILDING,** it looked like the end of BIG *everything* for Hogg, Hogg, *and* Hog.

Unless . . .
those big three
pigs could come
up with another
BIG BRILLIANT IDEA!

But, what?

"O-ink?"
  "Oooo-ink?"
  ". . . ink?"

Things looked bleak
for Hogg, Hogg, and Hog.
Things looked *very*
bleak indeed.

Then,
Hog remembered the
simple times . . .
down in the mud . . .
back on the farm.
With Sheep.
Duck.
Frog.

HOG looked at
HOGG,
 who looked at
HOGG,
 who looked at
HOG.

"Baa?"
"Quack?"
"Ribbit?"

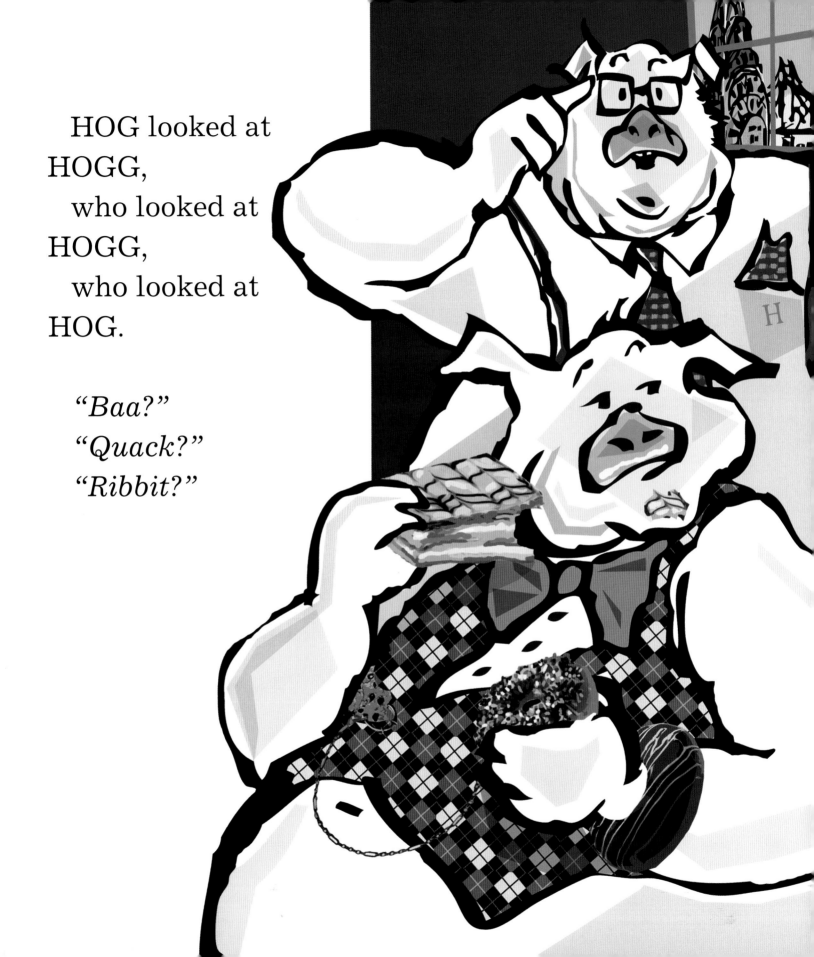

"OINK!"

"HOGG, HOGG, *and* HOG have done it again!

"They are still the most *famous*, fabulous, successful **BIG PIGS** ever to leave the farm and make it in the **BIG CITY**.

"What's the new *oink*, you ask?

BAA! QUACK! RIBBIT!

"That's right! Amazing! Genius! *Brilliant!*

"*How* do those three pigs keep coming up with these **BIG IDEAS?**"

The *very* next
morning, a
small red pickup
drove into the
**MIDDLE OF
THE
BIG CITY,**
and stopped
in front of the
BIGGEST BUILDING.

Up the elevator to
the top floor went . . .
Sheep,
Duck,
and Frog.

"Sorry.
Hogg, Hogg,
or Hog never
sees *anyone*
without
an *appointment."*

They were shown *right in*.

Hogg, Hogg, and Hog looked at Sheep, Duck, and Frog, who looked *right back* at Hogg, Hogg, *and* Hog.

Well, what else could those Three Big Pigs possibly say but . . .

"Oink?"

And now,
IN THE MIDDLE OF THE BIG CITY, ON THE TOP FLOOR OF THE BIGGEST BUILDING, it's very, very, *very* **BIG BUSINESS** at . . .

"Hogg, Hogg, Hog,
and *Partners* . . .
please hold.

"Hogg, Hogg, Hog,
and *Partners* . . .
please hold.

"Hold, please.
That line is *busy*.
One moment.

"*Sorry*.

"Hogg, Hogg, Hog,
or Partners *cannot* be
disturbed. . . ."

"They are *all* working on **NEW,** *brilliant,* very **BIG** ideas."